YEAR ONE

YEAR ONE

A WHISPER HOUSE PRESS ANTHOLOGY

EDITED BY STEVE CAPONE JR.

CJ ERICK   JONATHAN REDDOCH   HFJ BALLARD
VAL CHATINDO   J NEIRA   JAMIE JANAZIAN
PAUL LONARDO   JEN MEIRISCH   LIAM HOGAN
BEN MATTHEWS   THEODORE HILL
ERIN DAWKINS

FROM THE EDITOR'S DESK

Hello, spooky people, from the desk of the Whisper House Press editor-in-chief, publisher, chief marketer, lead designer, contract negotiator, and all-around average guy Steve Capone.

The book you're holding is assembled from the first year of whisper housepress.com's monthly featured stories. I want to thank you for picking up the volume and for checking out the free stories we host in perpituity on our website.

I always aim to be more transparent than you've come to expect from other publishers, and the [very brief] story today is of this anthology.

Amid the launch of two other anthologies in the fall of 2025, I determined I'd be wasting an opportunity if I don't take the stories I've already edited for our website and gather them into a collection. I bought a cover from Ruth Anna Evans and set to work offering new contracts with additional considerations (read: $10 payment beyond the original $10 purchase price) for the contributing authors' permission to include their shorts in this *Year One* anthology.

The anthology is forward-looking. *Year One* implies there'll be a *Year Two*, a *Year Three*, and so on. I hope to do this until I'm old, decrepit, and then I hope to continue after I expire. (I'm still troubleshooting this last bit of planning.)

If you like the idea of learning how the sausage is made, so to speak, with regard to publishing horror novellas, anthologies, web stories, and the like, drop by WhisperHousePress.com for more *Notes from the Editor* or *From the Editor's Desk* (or whatever I'm calling them) entries. There, I post everything from the contracts I use with my authors to my business plans and dreams to notes about mistakes I've made and from which I've learned.

Thank you so much for reading. I'm fully aware you have at your disposal a limited and unknown quantity of life-minutes and you've dedicated at least a few of them to reading some stuff my contributors and I have put together.

I appreciate you.

Steve
Salt Lake City, December 2025

CONTENTS

JANUARY: WHISPER HEIGHTS INDEPENDENT SCHOOL PANEL (WHISP) NEWSLETTER

CJ ERICK

CJ Erick's stories have been published by *Brilliant Flash Fiction, WMG Publishing, Camden Park Press,* and others. His short fiction received a recent Pushcart nomination and inclusion in *The Best Small Fictions 2023* anthology. He writes in multiple genres, publishes novels in a space fantasy series, and dabbles in poetry. He lives in the Dallas area with his wife and their rescue superhero dog Saber-Girl, calls his sourdough bread starter "Ursula" (K. Le Guin), and—for a Midwest Yankee—cooks crazy-good Cajun food. MFA 2022. Kenyon Review Fiction Workshop 2024.

———

APRIL, 2025

ANNUAL POETRY COMPETITION

The annual poetry competition scheduled for May has been postponed until further notice. The two teachers who facilitate this competition have taken unexpected leaves of absence for unrelated personal reasons. To address the rumors circulating among students, they've each given permission to share the generalities: Mrs. Henson is under rest orders and observation, and well-wishes may be directed to her at the mental rehabilitation ward at Mt. Carmel Hospital. Miss Stephens is currently undergoing treatment at an unnamed facility and is not receiving messages. Parents concerned about rumors of "verses summoning demons from the Gates of H_ll" are advised not to take these rumors seriously and are reminded that young teenagers have overactive imaginations.

FURNACE INSPECTION

Merriman HVAC Specialists are currently conducting an inspection and repair of the main air furnace system. Teachers and students had reported "strange wailing" noises coming from the school basement before dark smoke issued from the system vents. Initial findings have uncovered nothing unusual, although a small amount of green oozing material permeates the ductwork. Additionally, system controls were found to have been adjusted by unknown parties, but student suggestions the system might be "haunted" should not be taken seriously.

A final report on the HVAC system is expected shortly.

SPELLING BEE RESULTS

Alexandra Plinska has won the annual 8th Grade spelling competition after successfully spelling the word "catharsis" to claim the prize. After the field was reduced to five contestants from the original forty, Michael Thomas was eliminated after misspelling "toxicity," two other contestants fell ill and withdrew, and a fourth was disqualified due to her absence the day of the finals, which followed an unfortunate restroom accident the day before.

Note: Please report any information about the whereabouts of Timothy Jones, the winner of the 7th Grade Competition, to the county sheriff's department.

Alexandra recently moved to Whisper Heights from St. Petersburg, Russia with her parents Ilya and Ivan. The Plinskas have requested no inquiries into past or present occupations be answered but report having left behind "a large family" in their home country and have asked that questions about their residence's location by unknown parties be reported to the county sheriff's office.

SPORTS JAMBOREE

The annual sports jamboree was a huge success, with not one, but seven state record performances by school athletes from the four-county area. New records were set in girls' high jump, boys' long jump, girls' and boys' 400-meter dashes, girls' shot put, and both the girls' and boy's 100-meter freestyle swims. Please note that urine samples collected from all event winners are due by Friday May 1 at the request of the State Committee for Athletic Means and Measures (SCAMM).

Note: The county sheriff's office requests that athletes refrain from sending them any additional urine samples.

SCIENCE FAIR

Lara McMelson has won the annual Spring Science Fair competition with her dancing Artificial Intelligence Computer Model, which featured videos of dancing cats. Several other AI image-generation projects were disqualified. Images and videos have been reviewed extensively by art teacher Mr. Wormsley and PE teacher Mr. Petersen. They report any resemblance to persons living or dead in the offending materials were purely coincidental, especially those depicting other faculty members.

Note: Chemistry projects will be banned from future science fair competitions after one team "accidentally" produced designer steroids. Unfortunately, the exhibit was robbed, and any information about the whereabouts of taken materials should be turned over to the county sheriff's office.

SCHOOL COMPUTER SYSTEM HACK AND RANSOMWARE

We're pleased to report that all student records have been released by the Rude School ransomware group after a nominal payment was made. Perpetrators offered assurances our students' files would not be targeted again. The two Commodore 64 school computers are being upgraded as part of the expanded school budget. All proceeds from the annual carnival for the Future Business Architects (FUBAR) will be used for these upgrades.

DISCIPLINARY SUMMARY

- Two sixth-grade students have been suspended pending investigation of selling controlled substances after a large bag of money was found in the locker they shared.
- An investigation is underway into a suspicious envelope containing a white powder received by math teacher Mr. Walters. For those concerned, Mr. Walter has been taken off the ventilator and is expected to make a full recovery. At this time, his return date is unknown. Any information about the source of this envelope or about the nature of the substance should be reported to the county sheriff's office.
- Drama coach Mr. Lupus is offering a $50 reward for information leading to the return of a FedEx package taken from his vehicle in the school parking lot. Discretion is requested as the item taken was a special gift for an acquaintance. A reward bonus is offered if the package is returned unopened.

Now Hiring!
Full-time and substitute teachers
Bus drivers
Janitor
Utilities operator

FEBRUARY: ANNIVERSARY SURPRISE

JONATHAN REDDOCH

Jonathan Reddoch is co-owner of Collective Tales Publishing. He is a father, writer, editor, and publisher. He writes sci-fi, fantasy, romance, and especially horror. He's a prolific flash fiction author but also writes poetry and short stories. He has been working on his enormous sci-fi novel for over a decade and would like to finish it in this lifetime, if possible. He's from southern California but lives in Salt Lake City. Notable works are included in *Deluxe Darkness*, *Darkness 101: Lessons Were Learned*, and *This Isn't the Place*. Find him on Instagram @JonathanReddochAuthor or at CTPfiction.com

———

Larry arrived home late with a big bottle of warm budget champagne in hand.

"Van, I'm home!" He entered their modest one-bedroom apartment to find a trail of rose petals leading to their boudoir.

A hundred yellow candles surrounded their marital bed.

"Babe!" he called, "You outdid yourself. So romantic!"

Vanessa called from the bathroom, "Put the hood over your head. Take off your clothes and lie on the bed!"

He did as bidden, stripping out of his suit and putting the black bag over his head. He opted to keep just the necktie.

"You ready for me?" Vanessa asked.

He felt her nude body straddle his hips. Her cold fingers took his hands and strapped them down with rough cord—then his ankles.

He chuckled. "Kinky stuff, babe." He felt Vanessa lean in.

She breathed: "Happy anniversary, lover!"

"You too, babe."

She tightened his tie like a noose.

"What's the safe word?" he managed to choke.

She hissed, "To correctly pronounce it, you'd need to split your tongue in two."

MARCH: RAT

HFJ BALLARD

HFJ Ballard is an eclectic writer from what was once rural Utah. He is the author of the novel Monster and the creator of the comic Miles to Go. Ballard believes there is no meaning deeper than a moment of beauty without purpose.

———

Teeth brushed, jammies donned, stories read. Bedtime routine complete, Mr. Jayworthy of Jayworthy & Co. tucked his three daughters into three beds, kissing each on the head.

"Daddy," the youngest daughter said. "Why does the rat play the piano every night?"

Her father shuddered. "The rat?" he asked, left eye twitching ever so slightly.

"In the drawing room."

"Of course it *would* be in the drawing room," he said. "That's where the piano is."

"But why does he *play* the piano?"

"Who?"

"The rat."

The girl's father shuddered again. "Couldn't you say it was a mouse?" he asked.

"No," the youngest daughter replied.

"Why not?"

"Because it's a rat."

"Perhaps a very large mouse?" her father said, glancing toward the door.

"It's not a mouse," the daughter said. "It's a rat."

"How do you know?"

"Because of the song."

"Song? What song?"

The little girl took a child-sized breath and sang in a warbling, minor tone:

When the rat man plays his tune, then come we into your room. Gobble you up and slurp you down. One two three, we walk around.

Loved ones never know the truth of what has happened to their youth. One two three, and one's away, here but gone, and gone to stay.

Upside, downside, inside out. They never shout, they never shout.

One and two, there's just one left. Tomorrow night, our final theft.

Come quietly into the night.

Come quietly into the night.

The silence following her song scratched at the dark corners of the room.

"Well, there you have it," her father said, each syllable pushing itself through molasses and tripping on the uptake. "It's not a rat at all, but a rat *man*."

"Is that very different?"

"Is that... Where did you hear all this, anyway?" the girl's father asked.

"The shadows." The youngest daughter looked toward the far wall, past her sisters who were sitting on their respective beds, staring at nothing.

Their father looked in that direction as well.

The two older girls were statuesque, did not explain their sister's fantasies—did not even move their matching midnight eyes.

"I think you need more sleep," the man said. He kissed his youngest daughter once more on the forehead and fled the room with hesitantly lurching steps.

The lights clicked off, the shadows advanced to take its place.

In the drawing room, a creature that might have been a rat and might have been a man sat at the old Steinway & Sons piano, roughly laying tombstone-grey claws on scuffed keys.

In the bedroom, the shadows did a marionette dance past two empty beds.

APRIL: THE EGG TREE
VALARIE TENDAI CHATINDO

Valerie Tendai Chatindo is a University of Zimbabwe biochemistry graduate, now a writer and sexual health & awareness educator. She's a regular contributor for The Kalahari Review, Enthuse Magazine, The Diplomat Zimbabwe and EarGround. Her work has also appeared in Pink Disco Magazine, Creepy Pod, Agbowo, Omenana, Writer's Space, and Literary Yard. Her short story "Sheba," was shortlisted for the African Cradle African Heroines literary prize and her work published in Povo Africa's Nehanda Reimagined. The twenty-eight-year-old writer resides in Harare, Zimbabwe with her cat, Muffins. She runs her own literary platform, Shumba Literary Magazine.

Note from the editor: This story has been nominated by the Publisher for a Pushcart Prize.

———

in loving memory of Zie

———

Location: Uzo

Harvester 4009 POV:

You can always tell when an egg is *ripe,* so to speak.

I couldn't tell you the exact science except that... *if you know you know. And when you know, you know.* Well...

...we know.

Each day we set out, baskets in hand. Fingers cautiously prying through the sharp and polished ends of the many thorns decorating the Acacia trees designated by some greater authority, for whatever reason, to bear the prized fruit. Breath held and muscles taut with concentration and great contraction, we move through the millions of rowed trees. Gently handling the task at hand, aware of our cosmic responsibility. Conscious that we are accountable for an entire ecosystem.

The universe.

We cannot be arrogant. We cannot be selfish. Some would call us robots. Others? Mindless freaks. Still, we cannot afford to debate your opinions of us. We only live for the task at hand. Our cosmic duty as I have said before. This seemingly menial task, the core of not only ours but the entire human existence. A seemingly menial task we take seriously.

No mistakes. No room for error.

The mantra we chant each day as we set out. The mantra we chant as we pick our way through the fruit.

No mistakes. No room for error.

The mantra we chant even in our dreamless slumber in a world where the sun never sets. A world where the sun simply fades to a dark green hue signaling the end of yet another "day." This nameless realm with no concept of time nor the seasons.

A place where we have no identities or names.

Here we simply are the *harvesters.*

Soul 0078667445764347744 POV:

I've always wondered what one person's life is worth in the grand scheme of the universe. Whether our actions and lives matter. I'm a Christian and we talk about predestination. That God has mapped out a person's entire life before he has been conceived.

'I knew you before you were formed in your mother's womb'

I often wonder whether that statement is layered. Because in as much as I'd like to believe in the idea of an afterlife. One where we are afforded another chance to live out our humanity minus the perversions of this world I also have read other spiritual texts that imply that we are part of a collective consciousness. That we will simply be reabsorbed into that one thing when we die.

And so when God says he knew us, isn't he somehow talking about his own self awareness—because, of course, he knows himself?

But hey. This is all speculation. And I'm Christian, so I shouldn't even be thinking these kinds of thoughts.

Harvester 4009:

Is one person's life important in the so-called grand scheme of things?

In my many existences I may have debated the idea. Perhaps in one I was deeply spiritual and as such was absolutely certain that it was so, and then in another I was fixated by the mundane necessities of life and considered it not to be. Either way. Now I am, without a doubt, sure a life matters. For one existence sets the framework for the next and what comes after.

Every life matters.

Today, like any other day, I'm up just as the sun's brightness intensifies. I pull on my black robe, mantra leaving my lips in a whisper, my mind fixated on one particular fruit.

I shouldn't… *but I can't help it.*

Though the idea is absurd, I find myself attached to it. I mean, of course my attachment is absurd, considering that we handle thousands of fruit each day. Why, then, should I recall one fruit's exact location or recount the number of freckles dusting its delicate brown shell? In a realm where I'm forbidden from sentiment and dissuaded from attachment, how do I find myself drawn in by one meaningless fruit?

Meaningless?

Hahaha! Who am I kidding? Of course I am attached. Of course I am interested.

I am interested.

I am invested.

Yet the very act of caring is the greatest defiance to my vow. As harvesters, our job is never to ask, never track, never to think—but to simply harvest. And who are we if not the most meticulous and most callous lot from the human population? Our focus is reminiscent of characteristics most associated with the Autism spectrum. The world sees it as a limitation, but here it is a coveted quality, unhindered by the emotions and distractions that plague the average being.

Am I a hypocrite then? A fraud, liar, an imposter? I chose this life, no one forced me. I vowed not to feel. I vowed not to care. I vowed not to be enamored.

Yet…

I've had my eye on this particular one. I'm haunted by its existence.

Freckled and a deep brown. Just about ripe. Almost there…

I will not be the one to pick it. We are rotated through different orchards every week and someone else will be the one to pull it from its stem, without any thought or sentiment. So I will savor this time. I will allow myself to be pulled by the chords of familiarity which have captivated me. I am Judas and steal forbidden caresses when no one is looking, rousing memories, projected like a tape in my mind.

I have aroused your curiosity, I'm sure.

You see, this fruit you see was planted by me. Because I too was once just another piece of fruit from the Egg Tree. This egg is mine.

Soul 00006565664545445475666 POV:

It happened again.

That dream where I find myself flung into a deep pit only to wind up pulled out to another side, to a world where my dead family members surround me, concerned looks on their faces. To a world where after the panic and anguish of being pulled, I'm suddenly at peace, overcome by a tranquility I can't explain.

A premonition of death?

I'm not superstitious. If I were, death isn't taking me anytime soon. My entire life has been a sort of tragedy: My parents died before my third birthday, my only sibling following soon after. I was not only orphaned but lived as a stranger in this world passing from home to home, relative to relative, as might a shadow.

No.

I won't end up a tragedy.

I have dreams, ambitions, and goals. I have aspirations of carrying on the legacy of those who have gone before me whose time was cut short. I have dreams and cannot die.

Yet…

Whispers and premonitions of death plague my sleep. I must pray the God I believe in is working harder than the devil chasing after me. That black hooded figure won't get me.

Harvester 4009:

It's interesting how people die.

Each person's experience of death really depends on their faith—by what they believe. For those who believe in an afterlife in which deceased family members are waiting, that is their experience.

And the faithless?

Human beings are powerful creatures, able to manifest almost anything they believe. It becomes sad for the person who dies believing in nothing. For them, only darkness awaits. Many of these people are also secretly afraid, and dying is a traumatic experience for them.

I should probably also mention that each person sees their harvester as they pass on. I don't know why this is necessary. It only happens that way.

Even the faithless don't die alone.

Soul 00006565664545445475666:

I'm almost thirty, and I don't own a house or car. It's one thing for a woman to say this, but as a man the idea presents a whole set of problems. I want a family: a wife and children. But how will I afford them the life they deserve when I haven't even achieved the goals I set for myself?

In my teens, I imagined that by my current age I'd have achieved more by now. Man! I used to judge my older cousins for having done nothing commendable with their lives, but look at me today. What have I done?

I own my business, but it feels more like a WWE wrestling match trying to stay profitable. Zim is one big circus, and the circus master is a crazy psycho who can pull any kind of trick out of his ass.

I know I'm doing enough, yet I'm always hounded by the idea that I could be doing more. My friends insist I'm too hard on myself, but am I tough enough?

Val called the other day and told me I should be proud of myself.

"Proud of what?" I wanted to ask.

Proud of what…

God I'm tired.

Harvester 4009:

I should tell you about the sponge tree.

They say—and by "they" I mean those who've been here longer than I have—our masters told them when the sponge tree runs out of sponges, time will end. I don't know why a sponge tree holds such significance or why the universal clock determining our end chose to masquerade as a sponge tree. Why sponges? It is a beautiful tree.

You should see it.

Every so often, a collective moaning travels like a wave across this tiny planet. These are the wails of the harvesters and all the others on Uzo. The wave begins from those closest to the tree and ends with those furthest. We all wail each time a sponge falls.

You might think we have ceased to fear death, that we have embraced the fickleness of life. But are we not still human? Do we still not try to hold on to that with which we are familiar?

What will happen when the final sponge falls?

What will happen to life?

Will there still be eggs to harvest? Life to plant?

When an egg is harvested, the person existing in your world dies.

Their cosmic obligation is up, and it is time for them to begin a new existence.

After we harvest the egg, the Planters bury it in soil. The Gardeners then water and fertilize it, allowing it to grow into a tree that produces more eggs. In this way, one soul becomes hundreds and thousands and millions, and so it goes. Each egg is important.

Today I mark my egg, drawing a single dot on its shell. This initiates the dying process.

Dying often doesn't happen instantaneously. Instead, death is kind of heartless. In our world it takes a full day. In yours, it might take longer—much longer.

I wonder what they're doing at this exact moment? And how will they pass on—in their sleep? A tragic car crash? Either way, I will not be there to see it. Someone else will harvest my egg.

Soul 00006565664545445475666:

So much to do, and not enough time.

I'm always in a rush, and I don't know why. I guess I've always been this way. I always needed to do things quickly.

Tonight, though? I'm feeling good about myself.

I rarely do.

Tonight, everything feels right, like I'm going to be okay. I'm not saying I'm dying, but if I did in this very moment, I feel a certain amount of peace about it because I know I've lived life the best way I know how to.

I fall asleep with that clarity, and, even as I'm met by the black hooded figure in my dreams, I'm at peace.

Harvester 4009:

I watch as a harvester two rows ahead pries my egg from its stem.

It's all over. Just like that.

I sigh and turn back to my work, but not before I hear shouting. Everyone around me hears it, too. I see the boy running toward us. Gardeners mostly present as children. It's strange because the

Gardeners hardly come to the harvest fields due to the melancholy. The boy reaches our elder and gestures wildly.

All the harvesters are close enough to gasp when the elder drops his basket of eggs and runs off with the boy.

We never drop the eggs.

Soon, harvester after harvester follows.

I reach the basket with my egg and slip it into my own. I am alone in the fields.

The silence is different. Ghostly.

I follow the trail to the crowd and slip between shaking bodies.

When I do I look up at the tree that once held many beautifully and intricately colored sponges. Pinks, purples, and colors we do not have names for. The tree has looked that way for a while. For a while, only one sponge has remained in the sponge tree.

The shaking amongst the crowd intensifies before everyone stiffens. And as we watch the final sponge falls slowly to the ground.

MAY: SCARLETT'S STOVE

J NEIRA

J Neira is the child of a Mexican immigrant, who now lives a glorious hicklib life in Minnesota. They are a cozy horror author. They are a slush reader at Graveside Press, as well as an author there and at West Avenue Publishing. They were a semi-finalist for the 2024 Iridescence Awards and are the author of Raven's Dream. Their novel, The Haunting of Lola Barrera, is coming soon from Graveside Press.

———

Scarlett shivered as she stepped out of her van. Grey clouds coated the sky and flakes of snow peppered her hair and drifted toward the ground. Gripping her tool kit, she traipsed to the door of the restaurant. Christmas music and caroling blared from down the street. Colorful lights flashed and pulsed.

Her phone buzzed.

She rolled her eyes, knowing it was her family texting her, again, reminding her it's Christmas Eve and she shouldn't be working. But the money offered for this job was too good to pass up. She needed it.

Scarlett stood outside the restaurant, furrowing her brow. Darkness shrouded the interior. A scrap piece of paper had been taped to the door. Ignoring the text, she lit the note with her phone light.

"No one can turn off the stove."

Scarlett expected to see the person who had hired her, but there was no sign of them. Distant laughter and clinking drinks reminded her people were busy celebrating the holiday.

She pursed her lips tried the door. That it was unlocked surprised her. Looking around, she got the sense no one had been here for a while. Chairs sat stacked atop tables. The only light in the place was from the dancing flames of the stove in the kitchen. Light stretched along the walls. But the place was empty.

Scarlett blocked her nose to the pungent smell of gas intermingled with congealed pasta sauce. She skirted the tables and crept into the kitchen, frowning at the fingers of blue and orange flames.

As she flicked on the lights, the kitchen exploded into view. She opened the oven. Nothing inside, apart from old charcoal and dust. Scarlett bent. Under the troublesome stove, an array of blue, red, and black wires and cables fed through the floorboards, plunging into the basement below.

Maybe a pilot-light thing.

She huffed in frustration, realizing she had to find her way into the basement, under the stove. She snatched her tool kit and trudged downstairs, descending. The floorboards creaked, and the whole space smelled of mold.

Her face had flushed from the heat of the problem stove, and she was already sweating, so she pulled off her jacket to get to work in her tank top. She opened the power board and flicked off the power and turned a knob to kill the gas.

She headed back upstairs to re-evaluate the scene, but the stove still burned. Frowning, Scarlett grabbed her stool, trudged back down, and grunted as she reached for the blue cords tangled from the ceiling, yanking them from the outlet. Sparks flew.

Upstairs again, Scarlett found the stove continuing to burn.

"What the hell?" she muttered, leaning against the kitchen door, wiping sweat from her forehead.

The stove flames flickered as if mocking her.

Back in the basement, now thoroughly perplexed, she grabbed her wire cutter. With an *oof*, she reached up and cut the red wires, then pulled them from the tangled web of other cords. She grabbed some replacements. She connected the replacement wires to the power source and then the back of the stove. Scarlett noticed, all at once, the Christmas carol from down the road had increased in volume. The children were screaming. She flinched and then grimaced as their voices grated against her eardrums.

She marched back upstairs to check if she'd finally killed the stove. But of course, even her latest trick had proven fruitless.

"Fucking stove! Argh!" She felt her cheeks flush again. Her usual approaches weren't working. Hours stretched by as she continued to work the problem. Still, the stove refused to quit.

Scarlett didn't give up. She rearranged plugs, circuits, and called the power company.

Nothing worked.

Eventually, a sliver of the moon peeked out from behind the clouds. The carolers had finally left for home. Bar lights winked out. Only the colorful decorations twinkled in the square outside the restaurant. She checked her watch: midnight. She sighed, wiping the oil and soot from her hands with a cloth.

Clearing her mind with some deep breathing, Scarlett slumped back down into the basement. Her skin crawled. Her hair plucked up. An icy draft brushed past her. Loosened strands of her long hair, now haggard and tangled, tickled her nose. A shiver spider-walked down her spine. For a split second, Scarlett heard the children singing "Carol of the Bells," completely out of tune.

The heat returned as if it had never left. So, too, did the silence.

She shook her head. It was late, and she was tired. But she wasn't about to give up.

Grunts and groans crawled from her throat as she snipped wires and flicked switches.

Nothing. Nothing. Nothing.

The flames taunted her with angry, orange claws. She leaned against the kitchen wall, tapping her forehead against the plaster in frustration. A greasy, delicious smell wafted into her nose. She whirled, eyebrows furrowed.

Scarlett yanked open the oven door, and steam billowed out. She jerked backward and waved her hand to disperse the vapor. Her pulse quickened.

A slice of pizza burned on the oven's top rack. The cheese bubbled, a blackness spreading over the crust.

Scarlett blinked.

It hadn't been there when she'd arrived.

"Hello?" she called around the restaurant, glancing over her shoulder.

No one responded, of course. It was well past midnight. Had Scarlett locked the door? Some kids must've snuck in to prank her. She grabbed some oven mitts and carefully removed the pizza. Even with the mitts, a searing heat burned through the fabric and scorched her skin. She yelped. Her heart hammered. She flung the pizza, splattering melted cheese against the wall. It slid, squelching onto the tile floor.

Her eyes prickled with frustrated tears. She wiped them away. Scarlett refused to cry over a stove.

Her eyes grew heavy, and her vision clouded. Still, she continued working.

The wind picked up, whispering against the restaurant's windows. The silence from the carolers and partygoers became heavier.

Careful not to touch the jumping flames, Scarlett grabbed hold of the oven with gloved hands and dragged it away from the wall. At once, the oven door slammed shut, she yelped, and she slipped on the grease pool that had appeared underfoot. Her hand flew out, catching her fall for an instant before giving way.

Scarlett crashed to the floor, her other hand awkwardly and only partially breaking her fall. A harsh crack preceded pain exploding in her wrist. Her back screamed. She examined her wrist and winced. It might not be broken, but the pain ricocheted up her forearm. Her tears triggered rage. She grabbed a stewpot from the counter and hurled it across the room, growling. The pot slammed into the wall, crashed to the floor, and rolled once.

She rubbed her eyes until she saw stars and bright colors. As she drew herself back to reality, the oven door creaked back open. Slowly. As if invisible hands were inching it open.

Something small twitched in the fire. Hairy digits, each an inch long, peeked out, and hugged the edge of the oven. Scarlett froze and squinted. Out crawled a spider. Its legs pitter-pattered down the side of the oven and along the floor. "Huh?!" she gasped. Color drained from her face. An icy draft oozed from the flaming oven.

She peered at the spider. It paused, staring right back at her. Scarlett could count its eight eyes on a body much larger than that of any spider she'd ever seen. Its eyes were pools of oblivion.

She stared too long, and the spider flinched. She leapt backward.

Then the oven made a strange noise. *Tick, tick, tick.* It came from inside, no louder than a clock.

The spider twitched with every *tick.* Scarlett scrambled to her feet, heart thundering and mouth agape.

She gripped the doorframe and watched, entranced.

The spider danced to the ticking until the sound stopped and the creature collapsed, apparently dead.

And yet, the stove still burned.

Scarlett gave her head a shake, convinced the exhaustion was causing hallucinations.

She nearly crawled back downstairs, resetting her efforts once more. Her eyes glazed over as she laid out her tools on the bench, frowning at the mess of wires before her. She blew out her cheeks.

Her footsteps echoed as she climbed onto her stepladder and pulled every wire out again, including the new ones. The restaurant plunged into absolute darkness when she shut off the main power again. Scarlett knew in her gut nothing would work. But still.

She climbed the stairs again.

Once more finding the orange flames billowing like scarecrows in the wind, she released a scream—a pitchy, groaning yell. She cursed the stove anew.

A shadow shifted behind the oven, startling Scarlett. Half a moment later, she'd convinced herself it was a shadow from the flames.

Scarlett clenched her fists. Her breathing was heavy, and sweat dribbled down her temple as the rage coursed through her veins, flushing hot in her cheeks. Muttering to herself like a mad person, she marched out of the restaurant and grabbed the sledgehammer from her van. She was too enraged to notice the swirling snow, the singing wind, and the liquid night sky.

Scarlett was exhausted, and the sledgehammer's head screeched as she dragged it along the floor, through the restaurant, and into the kitchen.

But she didn't even grimace.

Instead, she mustered every ounce of her strength and swung the sledgehammer. *Umph!* The stove protested as metal smashed into metal.

Scarlett hit it again.

And again. And again.

She growled. "FUCK!" The crashes of the blade against the metal reverberated off the walls and sparks flew. Her yells and the crashing material built to a roaring, ear-splitting crescendo.

At last, the adrenaline dissipated. She dropped the sledgehammer, and her shoulders drooped. Her watch passed three o'clock as she slid to the floor against the wall opposite the stove and dropped her head into her hands.

A Christmas carol echoed—a high-pitched, tinny noise. Her arm hairs stood on end. She held her breath. The music was coming from inside the oven.

Her pulse again ricocheted through her ears, blood pounding, and her pupils dilated.

Something was very wrong.

The oven tremored as if someone were shaking it. The metal shelves and interior fan rattled.

Scarlett screamed. Her heart clubbed against her ribs. Every instinct told her to run, but her feet were concrete. She remained rooted to the spot.

The Christmas carol continued floating from inside the oven. Finally, it stilled. The door snapped open.

A strangled scream tore from Scarlett's throat as a human hand reached out from inside the oven. The stubby, bony fingers were calloused and scratched. But they were the hands of a child. Christmas tree lights tangled around their fingers, pulsating.

"What the—?" Scarlett gasped, and a giggle escaped from the person emerging from the oven. It was a playful giggle. The creature appeared as a young girl, wearing a torn, ragged Christmas dress and a dirty Santa hat. Her lips curled into a grin. Her eyes glinted with nothing but hunger.

A scream caught in Scarlett's throat as the girl reached for her. She flinched away. But something about this girl drew her in. Scarlett couldn't help it. She grabbed the girl's hand.

The girl was singing "Carol of the Bells." While it the creature held her tightly, its skin melted away, like wax from a candlestick.

The scream Scarlett had been holding ripped from her throat. A shadow—demon who had worn the girl as clothing oozed from the melted mess and overwhelmed her.

Scarlett's scream was cut short. She collapsed and was pulled forward.

Soon, the stove's flames—at last—ceased.

JUNE: EMPLOYEE OF THE YEAR

JAMIE JANAZIAN

Jamie Janazian is a short-fiction horror writer. Her first collection, The Woman in the Walls and Other Stories, was published in late 2024. When she is not reading or writing, Jamie enjoys spending her time hiking, hoarding tea, and crocheting.

———

I stared, mouth dry, heart pounding, at the message from my boss—that awful combination of words my coworkers and I always prayed we'd never see: "You're in the running for Employee of the Year."

To send something so callous via email was just rubbing salt in an already open wound.

My eyes glazed over the wall of text that followed. I didn't need to read the details—I'd cleaned enough of the prior winners off the walls and ceiling of the soundproofed break room to know exactly what winning the award entailed.

After that initial, deep pang of fear faded, denial flooded in to take its place.

I wasn't just hitting my sales quota, I was *blowing it out of the damn water*—selling big ticket items daily. I never forget to place the stickers with my barcode on the products, either, so when my customers check out and the items scan at the register, the sales should always link to my employee ID.

We don't receive commission—there are other "incentives" to keep our sales up. I hadn't been watching the numbers because I knew I was making sales left and right. In short, I've never dreamt I was at risk.

It must be a glitch with our computer system, I decided with a nervous laugh as I closed the email. It *had* to be—something IT could probably sort out in no time.

When I finally regained control of my legs, I wobbled to my manager's office.

There was no miscalculation, he assured me. It *was my* employee ID at the bottom of our rankings.

"The barcodes never lie, Graham." He didn't bother making eye contact.

I was circling the drain, figuratively, and if I didn't get my shit together, I'd be circling it literally soon enough.

I begged my supervisor to review the camera footage—I knew he'd *see* me making those sales.

"Don't worry," he added, his smile vacant of anything remotely resembling happiness, "One way or another, we *all* contribute to the success of our company." I suppose by then he was long desensitized to the pleas of the desperate.

As I left his office, I assured myself this wasn't a death sentence.

Not yet.

I had another month until HR would calculate final standings. Before shit would get real. Before I'd be given a limp handshake and an empty "Thank you for your devotion to the company" and led down the hallway to the break room. Before I'd meet what lives behind the usually padlocked door. Before I'd learn what it *truly* meant to sacrifice myself for the good of the company.

Word spread fast around the office.

Kevin gave me his smug, shit eating grin—maybe he thought with me out of the picture he'd finally have a shot with Elise.

Elise… I just desperately hoped hers wouldn't be the name drawn afterward—the employee selected to hose what's left of me off the break room floor and down the stained, rusty drain.

As required, I began parking in my newly designated space at the far end of the employee lot—the faded sign indicating "Reserved for Employee of the Year" nearly swallowed up by the encroaching tree line. This "perk" added an extra ten minutes to my walk to our store, and I dreaded that added time in the oppressive Texas heat. The rational part of me knew it was soon to be a moot point.

One way or another, in another month, I wouldn't have that parking spot. If I were lucky, I'd live to see another summer—long enough to see some *other* poor bastard's car parked there.

If they hadn't already heard the news, when the rest of my coworkers saw my car in that space, they knew what it meant: Don't get too attached.

They started avoiding me. I didn't blame them.

We all knew what would be coming next if my sales didn't improve —it's the same thing that happens every time: We'd gather for the mandatory meeting on the closing night of the fiscal year, all eyes on the sorry son of a bitch who'd "won"—the room so quiet you could hear their muffled sobs. They'd receive what barely constituted a handshake from a manager who muttered, dead-eyed, his appreciation for their devotion to the company.

Next, the winner would be ushered to the break room to meet Corporate. No one tried to run—not after what happened in '19. Instead, the winner would always turn back, shooting us a desperate, final look—eyes pleading for someone, *anyone*, to intervene. And, of course, no one ever did.

Once the door closed behind them and that sound-proofed room swallowed up the last of their sobbing, begging—it was over. The rest of us would be sent home and I'd try to shower away that disgusting feeling, that sick sense of relief someone *else* was sent to their death.

Cal—the nicest guy—was the bottom performer two years ago.

He'd fallen so ill he'd nearly wasted away and eventually couldn't work. He must've thought that freed him from his contract. If he left and never came back to work, maybe he'd have been okay.

He must not have read the fine print in our hiring paperwork. Although, to be fair, if any of us had read it, we'd never have signed it.

Cal was a warning to the rest of us that, in our line of work, there's no quitting. If they have to track you down and find you (and I promise you they *will* find you)—well, wouldn't you prefer to go with your dignity, with the company compensating your loved ones—rather than be pulled, kicking and screaming, from your home and into the night?

Gina was employee of the year in 2023. Gina, with the kind smile, whom Kevin had set his sights on before Elise. And, just like Elise, she wanted nothing to do with him.

I still remember that day, the day they released the final numbers. The way Gina's mouth hung open in confusion, shock.

When she finally managed to form words again, she too had insisted there must have been some mistake. We all vouched for her to management—I'd personally seen her make innumerable sales.

Our manager simply reminded us: The barcodes never lie.

My name was the one drawn for break room duty that next morning, to pick up what remained of her smile along with her simple gold wedding band, both to be returned to her family. In one business week, they received a box containing a check, and everything left of her that wouldn't fit down the drain.

Once the numbers are finalized, your employee barcode slapped on an innocuous-looking pink slip, your fate is sealed.

Kevin, in all his years at the company, never parked on the far side of the lot. He never came close to becoming Employee of the Year, though he couldn't have sold a bottle of water to a man dying of dehydration. He is sleaze incarnate and doesn't have the charisma to mask it.

I never understood how he did so well, but I had myself to worry about and couldn't afford to think about him.

I worried over the glitch in the system. Any time I found myself in the break room, that ancient wooden door was an unwelcome reminder of my impending one-way trip.

I took special care to keep an eye on my sales, working my ass off, pulling double shifts. I ran the numbers as the end of month drew near, and couldn't believe it.

I was still dead last.

There had somehow been days when less than half of my sales were recorded to my employee number.

I didn't understand.

I waited for the opportunity to sneak into the manager's office to pull the footage myself.

I'd show the boss something had gone wrong with the calculations and the system was broken.

I finally got my chance. At first, I triumphantly watched myself make sale after sale—far more than had been credited to my account. For the first time in a month, I felt a sense of relief. I had evidence, and that had to count for something.

I switched feeds, to the camera nearer to the registers so I could confirm the codes were being scanned. I'd seen several scanned successfully, and reached to turn off the recording. That's when I saw it.

Saw *him.*

Kevin.

It was subtle. I didn't realize what he was doing at first, until I recognized the pattern. Even then, I had to rewind and watch again for it to click.

It happened for nearly half of my sales that day. I saw him intercepting the customers before they could check out—before I could get credit for my sales. And while he chatted them up, he discretely slapped his employee barcode over my own.

I confronted him that night—I was furious.

He just smiled and smugly gave me the line about barcodes never lying. He didn't give a shit he was sentencing someone else to death. Hell, maybe he *enjoyed* it.

Kevin had stolen credit for Gina's sales—and god knows who else's.

Fucking *Kevin.*

The day our numbers were to be finalized, he had the audacity to place his barcode over mine on a huge sale I'd made—he made no attempt at hiding it—right in front of me. He flashed me a grin as he did.

I caught up with the customers before they checked out and they kindly allowed me to peel the sticker off. I stuck it in my pocket to show my manager.

I pulled the video, too, and I stormed into his office, refused to leave until he watched it. I studied him as his eyes moved across the screen and if he was upset or shocked, he certainly didn't show it.

Finally, he met my eyes, and at the sight of the pain in his—well, for the first time, I felt a sense of relief.

Until I realized why he looked so miserable, whispering, "I'm sorry, Graham. Someone has to receive that award tomorrow. It's out of my hands."

I wordlessly handed him Kevin's barcode sticker, the one I'd peeled off.

He studied it for a long moment before he handed it back to me with a mere, "Why don't you hold onto this?"

I told Elise what had happened over lunch, and as much as I appreciated her outrage on my behalf, I was already resigned to it. I'd mainly wanted to warn her because I had a sick feeling she'd be the one Kevin went after next.

I'd be lying if I said I wasn't devastated when, that night, my boss called me into his office and informed me of the final standings. Yeah, I knew it was coming, but I guess it's just human nature to hold onto denial—hope—until the bitter end.

For what felt like an eternity, we stared at each other in silence. The presence of the pink slip of paper lying on the desk between us, said more than enough.

Finally, my eyes drifted down to the form.

He'd already signed, but the space where my barcode—the series of vertical lines spelling out my death sentence—should've been placed, was empty.

I never knew how this part went, since it always took place behind closed doors. No one who ever filled out that form lived to tell the rest of us about it.

"I need you to place a barcode here before I send the form to Corporate," he said.

I opened my mouth for one final, impassioned plea for my life, but he interrupted me. He spoke each word slowly, softly: "I'm leaving the room now. I need you to place *a* barcode here, before I send the form to Corporate." He stared at me for a long moment, waiting for my barely perceptible nod of acknowledgement, before leaving me alone in the office.

HR processed the paperwork, and they announced the Employee of the Year the next day.

Yes, I did feel a pang of guilt as I watched the smug grin fade, the blood draining from Kevin's face as he stared in shock at the outstretched hand of our manager—as he was thanked for his devotion to our company.

I felt it again as I watched him plead all the way to the break room, as our manager spoke to him the same mantra we'd all heard before: *The barcodes never lie.*

But I thought of Gina, of the countless others. And, by the time I heard the door slam behind him, my guilt had already gone, had been replaced with the relief of knowing the rest of us were safe.

Until next year.

JULY: THE MASSAGE

PAUL LONARDO

Paul Lonardo *is a freelance writer and author who has published numerous titles, both fiction and nonfiction. Paul has placed short fiction and nonfiction articles in various genre magazines and ezines. He is a contributing writer for* Tales from the Moonlit Path *and is an active HWA member.*

———

"You won't regret it," Nick said after convincing Scott to get the massage. "It will change your life."

"That's why I'm going," Scott told his friend. "My doctor says I need to make some changes in my life if I want to live to see my new grandson play little league. So I quit smoking and started a new diet. And if this massage is as good as you say, I can reduce my stress level on top of everything else. I'll be a whole new man."

"Susan is amazing," Nick added. "I don't know how she does it, but she not only invigorates your skin, but she awakens every muscle and nerve in your body. And it lasts for days. You'll feel every sensation like never before. I don't know how else to describe it. You just feel… alive."

Scott was excited when he called to set up an appointment and got a slot the following day. The timing couldn't have been better because he had been feeling tense the past few weeks, with persistent neck and shoulder tightness. He was looking forward to a relaxing massage.

When he arrived, he filled out a form, enumerating his underlying health or medical conditions: He checked the boxes for high blood pressure and a heart condition. He handed the paperwork back to the receptionist, who escorted him into one of the rooms.

"Once you get undressed, hop up onto the table, lie on your belly under the covers, and the massage therapist will be right with you," the woman told Scott.

The table was heated, and the soft, low-tempo music was so soothing it almost put him to sleep. He didn't hear anybody enter the room.

"Remain relaxed," came a voice. "I'm Susan, your massage therapist."

"Hello," he said, keeping his eyes closed and his head down in the facerest. "Nice to meet you."

Susan reported she'd read the information he'd provided and asked him what areas of his body he wanted her to target. Once she started working on him, they didn't speak again. She began on his upper spine and neck, gently manipulating the cervical vertebrae.

He couldn't help but moan in delight. When Scott's eyes flickered open, he caught a glimpse of the bottom of her legs in black Spandex and her white shoes, the kind a nurse might wear. He closed his eyes once more.

As she worked on his left arm, a sudden shooting pain radiated through his shoulders. He cringed, thinking she had triggered a nerve, causing the burning sensation. Every muscle in his body seemed to lock up, and he began perspiring profusely. As a wave of nausea swept over him, a tightness in his chest quickly intensified from discomfort to agony.

Then, all at once, the pain stopped and he only felt cold.

He knew he was lying on his back now. He didn't remember rolling over, and he wondered if he had blacked out.

His eyes were still closed, but when he tried to open them, he found he could not. As if in a nightmare from which he was on the verge of waking, he was unable to move. He could hear voices nearby, however, so he knew he wasn't alone.

What's happened? Can anyone hear me? Please.

"What happened to him?" one of the voices asked.

"He had a massive coronary during his massage," the other one answered. "Died instantly."

"How awful. At least he didn't suffer."

No. It can't be. You got it wrong. Scott summoned every last ounce of his will, and when a hazy light opened up in his field of vision, he tried even harder until two blurry figures appeared. They were standing directly over him, wearing white gowns and surgical face shields. They were doing something to him, but he couldn't see what it was.

"Oh, my God," one of them exclaimed. "His eyes just opened."

The other person laughed. "It's just a reflex. It happens all the time."

"That freaked me out."

"You get used to it. Hand me a scalpel, would you."

Wait. DON'T!

The blade made a soft crackling sound as it cut through cold flesh. There was no blood, but when the skin was pulled back it was red inside. The surgeon was handed an instrument that resembled a sturdy pair of scissors which crunched like splintering bone, and when it stopped, a breastplate had been removed.

This can't be happening! Why are you doing this to me?

The knife that was used next made wet squelching sounds. After several moments, the physician came away holding a large reddish-brown organ.

"Besides the liver, what else are we harvesting from the donor?"

"The corneas and temporal bones."

"Temporal bone? That's unusual."

"Yeah. It's for research. The donor's family has a history of inner ear disorders. So, let's each harvest a cornea, and then I'll show you how to extract the temporal bone?"

"Gladly. It feels like he's watching us. It's creeping me out.

No no no no.

Scott's eyelids were held open as a pair of steel blades descended, closer and closer, toward his eyes. Then, everything went black. Scott had only one sense remaining, and a couple moments later, there was a piercing crunching sound followed by terminal silence.

AUGUST: BREAK TIME

JEN MIERISCH

Jen Mierisch's dream job is to write Twilight Zone episodes, but until then, she's a website administrator by day and a writer of odd stories by night. Jen's work can be found in The Arcanist, NoSleep Podcast, Scare Street, and numerous anthologies. Jen can be found haunting her local library near Chicago, USA. She is an active member of the Horror Writers Association.

———

I'd been on the job for a couple of weeks when it happened.

I didn't see it coming. The only thing on my mind that night was that old-school clock up on the wall. I watched its plastic numbers flip until, finally, they read 2:00 AM.

Break time.

I set down the scanner, parked the pallet jack, and walked back inside from the loading dock. The forklifts' beeping echoed bleakly against the high ceilings and joined the droning buzz of the fluorescent lights, which bathed the racks in a jaundiced glow. A fat spider scurried beneath a discarded carton, inches from my sneakers.

Ace Warehousing might have been a cheerful place in the daytime. But during the night shift, the skylights, set in pairs in the corrugated metal roof, offered nothing but pitch blackness, staring down at us like the lidless eyes of some watchful demon.

The husky voice I'd come to detest came from behind. "Hey, hot mama." Nick maneuvered the forklift past me, leaning out of the cab with a leer. "Lookin' good."

My skin crawled. I rolled my eyes and kept walking.

Up ahead, Nick swerved toward something. The forklift bounced slightly as its wheels bumped over something on the ground. The sharp squeak and Nick's laughter told me all I needed to know.

I shuddered. The bastard had better get rid of the mutilated corpse this time. After my break, I'd check the supply closet for extra mousetraps.

Usually, I took my food and my textbooks to the picnic tables behind the warehouse. There, I could study under the floodlights. But tonight, rain pummeled the metal roof in a staccato symphony, so into the break room I went. There, I retrieved the cheesy bean-and-rice burrito I'd grabbed at Taco Bell on my way to work, popped it into the microwave for a minute, and dropped into a plastic chair.

Besides me, it was just Shirley, the middle-aged lady who spent her breaks with a soup spoon in one hand and a romance novel in the other, and Isabel, who knitted and listened to music. The only sounds were the clicking of Isabel's needles and the low hum of the vending machines. Joey, the sweet, odd kid who kept to himself, wasn't around. I yawned and contemplated a cup of the company-issued coffee, scalding in the pot and beckoning from across the room.

Whoops and hollers pierced the stillness. Through the break room windows, I spied Nick, driving the forklift. Tyler had perched on its prongs. Motor buzzing, the forklift rocketed past the door.

"Yeeee haw!" Tyler bellowed as they screeched around the corner.

I exchanged eye rolls with Shirley and Isabel. On a typical night, the boys would race the forklift down every aisle of the warehouse, gaining speed on the straightaways, taking each corner as fast as they could without tipping over. Then one of them would fork-lift the other up to the highest rack, where he'd grab the rope they'd tied there and swing down in an arc, Tarzan style, yodeling all the while.

We ignored them. No one had ever reported their behavior, as far as

I knew. The shift supervisor, Brenda, didn't bother coming in half the time, being salaried and all. We weren't working in the warehouse to make friends or enemies. Night shift paid twice as much as day shift, and we all needed that money for something.

"Hi, Isabel. Hi, Shirley." The chirpy voice took me by surprise.

My eyes darted upward. But it was only Joey.

"Hi Darcy," said Joey. "How ya doing today?"

I'd stopped being nervous around Joey after my first couple of days. At first, his twitching, that constant grin, and his dopey, overeager friendliness had put me on edge. I told myself he couldn't help it, that he was just a little different, that it was good of Ace to hire folks like Joey.

With his chubby cheeks, overbite, and light-brown hair sticking straight up from his head like bristles, Joey reminded me of a gerbil, more cute than scary. And he seemed to love everyone. If he wasn't gabbing to you about his favorite bands or reciting song lyrics with a savant's accuracy, he was asking to take a selfie with you. He was always grinning. Always.

"Hi, Joey." I risked a return smile. Probably I could smile without Joey interpreting it as an invitation, as Nick might have done.

Grinning back at me, Joey strolled to an empty table and pulled a Nintendo Switch out of the pocket of his cargo pants. His fingers punched buttons, pausing only to transfer Doritos from bag to mouth.

Down the hall, a gleeful howl, followed by laughter, echoed against the rafters.

On my first night at Ace, Nick and Tyler had tried to get me to ride the forklift with them at break time. Torn between wanting to make friends and wanting to avoid trouble, I'd declined. Tyler had looked disappointed, but he'd shrugged and left to start the night's races. Nick had looked petulant, like a child who hadn't gotten his way.

———

The next night was dry, the outdoor picnic area deserted. I settled onto my favorite bench and took out my sandwich.

"What up, girl," growled a husky voice.

Nick sat down on the bench next to me and immediately scooted closer.

I was acutely aware of his leg, three inches from my own. My nostrils filled with a mix of Nick's cheap cologne and whatever product he'd used to spike his bleach-blond hair. An earring glinted above his tattooed neck. Everything about Nick repulsed me, but rather than saying so, I hunched over my book in silence. Years of experience had taught me that telling him to buzz off would make me the bitch.

"That a good book you got there?"

"Mm-hmm." I stared at my biology textbook as if it contained a magic spell to banish creeps.

"Why dontcha give me your number," Nick said. It was more an order than a suggestion. "We can get together, maybe do something more fun than reading." His knees spread wider and his leg made contact with mine.

I edged away.

"No thanks," I muttered. "Just trying to study." I wondered if the warehouse had exterior cameras on this side of the building, and if so, whether anybody watched the footage.

"Studying," Nick said in the same tone of voice others might use to say *sewage*. "Come on, baby. You ain't got nothing to be afraid of."

I scooted some more. I was at the edge of the bench now.

"Mmm," Nick said, his eyes traveling everywhere on my body except my eyes, scanning my jeans and T-shirt like a snake deciding where to bite its prey. "I do love me some brown sugar." His fingers brushed my thigh.

I flinched and sprang awkwardly away from the table.

"Don't do that." Bristle-haired Joey stood in the doorway, arms folded, glaring at Nick. His face twitched more than usual, but his voice was clear, and for once, he wasn't grinning. "You stop that. Can't you see? Darcy doesn't like that."

I stared at Joey, open-mouthed.

Nick spat a dismissive laugh, but he was looking at Joey too. Maybe it was the lateness of the hour, maybe it was the floodlights lighting Joey's face from below, casting a huge shadow behind him, but Joey's brown eyes seemed beadier than usual—like those of a nocturnal creature stalking its prey.

"What?" said Nick, "You planning to make a move?" He slid off the bench and stood to face Joey. "Trying to get yourself a piece of that ass? Fat chance, dipshit."

Joey didn't move. I looked from one man's face to the other. Some unspoken signal seemed to pass between them. Nick took a step backward. Was this some sort of bro code I couldn't fathom?

"You go away," said Joey. "Leave Darcy alone." His arm jerked sideways, casting a giant-sized shadow behind him. The left side of his face twitched so hard that it looked contorted. His eyebrows folded into a V shape, which might have been comical, but then his throat started spasming. "Get lost," he said. "Get. *Get. GET.*" The sounds were guttural, rhythmic. They grew louder with each subsequent word until they were like the bark of a furious dog. Joey's other arm flung out. The shadows on the wall behind him were two enormous black wings.

"What the fuck," sputtered Nick. "Something is seriously wrong with you, dude." But he backed off. He shook his head, he grumbled insults under his breath, he accidentally-on-purpose clocked Joey on the shoulder on his way back inside—but he kept walking.

———

The next night, it rained again. Joey and Nick appeared to be back on good terms, both of them cruising on the forklift together with Tyler. All I could do was shake my head. I'd never understand men.

In the break room, as I chewed my bologna sandwich, I could hear all three of them horsing around up on the top shelves, up near the ceiling. Suddenly, their hollering was interrupted by a loud smack, followed by an ear-splitting scream of pain, and then silence. Shirley and I looked at each other, got up from the tables, and ran.

Nick lay on the floor, whimpering. Blood oozed across the gray concrete. The seep kissed the frayed edge of the broken rope, turning it lipstick red.

When the paramedics touched Nick's leg to lift him onto the

stretcher, his shrieks echoed off the metal ceiling, the canyon howl of a wounded wolf.

The next day, a new guy clocked in, and we never saw Nick again.

———

"Hi Darcy, how ya doing today?"

I glanced up to see Joey taking a seat at an empty picnic table with his Switch. The floodlights lit the side of his smiling face.

"Doing better now?" he asked me.

The dopey grin was the same. Or was it?

His left eye twitched. It might have been a wink.

SEPTEMBER: LIFE CHOICES
LIAM HOGAN

Liam Hogan is an award-winning short story writer, with stories in Best of British Science Fiction and in Best of British Fantasy (NewCon Press). He volunteers at the creative writing charities Ministry of Stories, and Spark Young Writers. Sci-Fi collection: A Short History of the Future (Northodox Press). Fantasy: Happy Ending Not Guaranteed (Arachne Press). More details at happyendingnotguaranteed.blogspot.co.uk.

————

My arm is tired, the baseball bat is slick with gore, and the light is fading fast. I try a swing with my left, but I make a meal of the strike (*You're hitting like a girl, Maggie!*). Accuracy and power are equally important, my father always said.

Whether this is the rapture or a zombie apocalypse doesn't matter. Same difference, far as I can tell. The dead are restless. As soon as I heard, I high-tailed it to the cemetery. I never got to say goodbye or do the things I should have done, and I wasn't going to miss a second chance.

I'd had to abandon the Honda in gridlock around Main Street and jog the rest of the way, giving returnees a wide berth, panicking at the thought I'd be too late. But I found his plot undisturbed, which was more than I could say for those of his neighbors.

If I'd been better prepared, as he would have wanted me to be, I'd have brought a head torch, and more than my by-now empty canteen of water. I didn't expect to wait this long. Maybe it's exhaustion, but as the bruised shadows gather I can almost hear him.

"You oughta consider your life choices, Maggie," he'd say in his lazy drawl. "Lookit where they got ya."

But they were never my choices, were they, Papa? And this is where they got me: waiting with my Louisville Slugger, waiting for the moment you claw your bastard way out of the grave.

OCTOBER: MOTHER KNOWS BEST

BEN MATTHEWS

Ben Matthews *is a physiotherapist who completed a Master of Writing through Swinburne University in 2021. He is a contributor to the Killer Creatures: Horror Stories with Bite Horror Anthology, Spawn 2: More Weird Tales About Pregnancy, Birth, and Babies, and a finalist in Dark Regions: Survive the Night horror writing competition. When he is not writing, he is drawing or riding his unicycle. He lives in Perth with his amazing wife who thinks horror stories are silly. Check out his website at bjcmatthews.wixsite. com/ben-matthews-author.*

Note from the editor: This story has been nominated by the Publisher for a Pushcart Prize.

———

"It could kill someone. Think about that!" Mrs. Ellis returns her attention to her cup of coffee, selects the tiny silver spoon on the saucer beside it, and stirs its contents.

The tiny utensil is made of pure, gleaming silver. Mrs. Ellis does not look up at me. She stares at her cup, stirring. Stirring. Her eyes follow the spoon, around and around. She holds the spoon upright. Pushes it in front of my face like a tiny silver STOP sign.

Mrs. Ellis uses the spoon to transfer sugar from an ornate silver bowl to her cup. She stabs the spoon into a dish of clotted cream. She stabs and twists, excising a perfect marble of yellow cream. She drops it in her cup.

Clink!

She stares at her cup, stirring, stirring.

Finally, Mrs. Ellis sighs. "I hope I am not asking too much." She places the spoon on her saucer.

Clink!

She sips from her coffee.

I take a sip from my water bottle.

Council policy says we must never accept food or beverages from people whose homes we visit. It is still rude that Mrs. Ellis does not offer, especially when I have to sit through her five-minute coffee-making routine.

Mrs. Ellis sits, stiff as a store mannequin.

I take a deep breath. *You do not make someone watch you prepare and drink your coffee unless you are playing mind games.*

"The hedges are an eyesore. And they are dangerous." She said.

"It's fine. As I said, we've—"

"It is an accident waiting to happen. There is no visibility on that corner."

"Mm."

"You're sure you cannot do any more?"

"We've issued them a notice. They have two weeks to respond."

"Two weeks is a long time."

An orange tabby slinks into the room. It skirts around the table, away from Mrs. Ellis, and lands between my feet. The pet looks up at me with a single green eye. In place of the other is a pink, ragged scar.

Mrs. Ellis scowls. "Winston! Go away! Shoo!" She stabs the tiny spoon at the cat.

Winston flees the room.

"I'm sorry," she said. "He really should know better."

"It's okay. I like cats. My uncle used to have one like him, poor thing."

"Poor thing?"

"It got its eye scratched out by another cat, too."

Mrs. Ellis purses her lips. "Two weeks is too long."

Clink!

The spoon lands on its saucer.

"People have no respect for the rules anymore."

I take a long, slow breath. There is no hazard. There is plenty of room on the road.

"No respect at all," she repeats.

"Please be aware we will address it appropriately," I said.

My job is to ensure that homeowners are compliant with maintaining their properties. Somehow, it has devolved into pleasing the Mrs. Ellises of the world.

Mrs. Ellis picks up her spoon again and carves a circle in the air before her.

Somewhere at the front of the house, a door slams.

"Door!" she snaps.

A boy's voice responds, "Sorry, Mother."

"We are in the tearoom!" she calls back. Then, to me: "People need to show some damned respect for the rules."

"I can ask this case be prioritized," I said.

Mrs. Ellis points her spoon at me. Looks me straight in the eye. "You're not just saying that?"

"No."

"I hope not!"

"Hi, Mother. Good afternoon, sir!" A boy of about ten stands in the doorway. Over his left eye is a black leather eye patch. Just a normal ten-year-old boy.

With only one eye!

I look away, quickly.

"Hello, Christian. Give your mother a kiss." She puckers her sour lips at him.

Christian obeys.

"Now, go to your room and do your homework. Understand?"

"Yes, Mother." He turns to me. "Good afternoon, sir!"

I nod, looking anywhere but his eyepatch.

Mrs. Ellis has her damned spoon poised in her fingers again. She raises it to her lips, pushes her pale white tongue out, and presses the side of the spoon's bowl to it. A bead of blood appears on her tongue. The edges of the silver utensil are razor-sharp.

Tenderly, Mrs. Ellis scoops the single drop of blood, a ruby in the bowl, and locks eyes with me. "I do not like disobedient boys. Disobedient boys grow up to be dishonest men. I hope you are not lying to me. My Christian used to tell lies, but now he is the perfect angel. Don't you think?"

NOVEMBER: A TASTE
THEODORE HILL

Theodore Hill (he/him) is a writer, librarian, and queer horror living somewhere on the East Coast of the US. He spends the majority of his non-work hours maintaining his recreational spreadsheet collection and regaling his friends and loved ones with deeply worrying story pitches. He can be found online at theodorehill.weebly.com.

———

He told himself it was just the stress. Once things calmed down, he'd cut the habit again.

Still, he stood in front of the sink and stared at the cratered mess of his face. He told himself it wasn't serious even as his fingers found their way to his lower lip and worried a scrap loose, pulling it free with a satisfying snap and the taste of metal on his tongue. He told himself he could stop at any time as he stared at the fragment of his skin, thin and translucent as a pastry flake, between his thumb and forefinger.

He dropped the scrap of skin down the stopperless drain in his bathroom sink, with the others.

His hand wandered to the back of his neck, fingernails grazing his scalp. Dozens of rice-sized scabs marred every inch of the surface already. Every time he found one, he'd work at it. Every near success sent a sharp, hot flush of agony ending in the satisfying slide of the loose bit of flesh dragging along adjacent hairs. These went in the sink's maw, too.

If he threw them in the trash, he'd have to face just how many small fragments of himself he'd picked free and discarded. Looking at his pocked and divoted cheeks, he'd rather not consider the lost volume. It was bad enough there was always blood under his fingernails. If he tossed the evidence down the sink, at least it would really be gone.

The rumbling from the drain was quiet, at first. So quiet, he didn't notice the sound until the pipe from thet basin to the wall distended like a bolus. Like the sink had found something hard to swallow or was choking. The pipe groaned one final protest and then the porcelain bowl of the sink cracked in two.

Before he could step back, a fleshy pipe shot out and coiled around his throat. It felt like a tongue, slick and muscular and prehensile, dragging his struggling body toward a widening mouth.

There were more tendrils. Dozens, *hundreds* more. Some were slender, like the one choking him, but others were broad and flat, covered in toothy, ovoid mouths like a dozen leeches made one flesh.

They were grasping. All of them wanted a taste.

He grasped for anything solid. His already bloodied fingernails cracked and splintered on the tile bathroom wall. The towel rod snapped off the wall in his grip. The first mouthy arm pressed its face to his, gnawing sharply at what skin remained.

When the leechthing pulled free, it took too much with it. The tentacle around his throat pulled him into the jaws of the mess of his sink. Shards of porcelain pressed in on his skin, the shrill shriek of his body rubbing along the wet surface briefly eclipsing the rumble of whatever lurked below.

When he tried to scream, a leechthing slithered between his lips, latching onto his tongue and gagging him with foreign flesh and hundreds of needle teeth. The slime-slick walls of the passage he was being dragged through compressed his shoulders, crushing his body ramrod straight. All he could do was wait and choke and hope and pray that whatever was waiting for him at the end of the tunnel had teeth enough to cut short his miserable, rib-cracking suffocation.

DECEMBER: FIRST KISS
ERIN DAWKINS

Erin Dawkins (she/her) received her MA in English with a specialty in Creative Writing from Wayne State University in Detroit, Michigan. Recent fiction has been published in Wild Greens Magazine, Flash Fiction Magazine, Five Minute Lit, Half and One and forthcoming in Sky Island Journal and Still Here Magazine. She recently completed her debut literary horror novel. In 2025, she received an Author's Fellowship from the Martha's Vineyard Institute of Creative Writing.

––––––––––

The man gazes at her with the curiosity of a hundred eyes. He leans into her and grazes his tongue over her lips. They feel dry and cracked, like clay.

She is in the shallows of the riverbank, surrounded by water lilies. Her body moves weightlessly with the perpetually lapping river.

He cups his hand around one of the heart-shaped pads holding the lilies like a tea cup and saucer, and then he stares at her for a long time. "Lily," he whispers.

Lily doesn't wince or shutter, as she can only lie still. Though something wakes inside her—something she yearned for while she was still breathing with life. When she sat along the river for hours, watching men and women, hand-in-hand, each couple awaiting their first kiss. She used to practice on her arm, goosebumps like mountains on her skin, imagining the moment when it would finally be her turn to be kissed.

As darkness fell, Lily found herself walking along the river, her fingers floating airily through thick, drowning fog. She approached a clearing to find a man and woman on a bench. Their lips drawn close together, hesitantly at first, as if they were never meant to touch, but when they do, it's as if their lips were never meant to part. Lily brings her face close to the woman's.

The man's heart pulsates like that of a wild animal, the cage of his chest barely restraining it.

Lily doesn't fight the urge to squeeze the man's heart and mute the noise, to strangle the universal emblem of love. Her arm leads, and soon it is inside his chest. The length of her arm is buried, and, slowly, she is inside him. Her entire body is one with his and she can feel his heart becoming less excited and more irregular.

Lily inhales.

The other woman's eyes are open and petrified. Her cheekbones and jawline rip through her graying, sunken skin. The buttons on the man's shirt pop, as the bones in his sternum and ribcage snap like dried sticks framing an expanding cavity. The woman's eyes, once suffused with terror, are now devoid of life. What's left of the woman shrivels and falls onto the seat of the bench like a shriveled balloon.

The man's hands cling to his broken chest as Lily leaves his body. She faces him, smiling with satisfaction. He looks at the bench, and then back at Lily, and begins tearing at his throat. His mouth is agape, gasping for the scream lodged like a sick lump. The scream is buried, silenced and stolen in the thick of a most terrifying dream. Lily watches as he flees, shrinking into the darkness.

Just then, Lily is overpowered as she begins to gasp for air herself. Her hands reach up around her neck. She is under the veil of murky water, recalling the nightmare of her own fate. Two thumbs press hard into the base of her throat. She reaches to the night sky from the depths of the water, unable to fight the force holding her down, burying her breaths like treasures lost below, never to resurface again.

———

It's night again when Lily finds herself at the riverside. The fog carries her to a man and woman on a blanket at the edge of the water. She watches them talk, laugh, and embrace each other with loving gestures. Just as they lean in for a kiss, Lily settles into the man's body.

The woman opens her eyes when she feels his hands swallowing her thin neck.

The man, *Lily*, opens his mouth wide and moves it to hers. His eyes are bedeviled as he inhales her life force, until only a shrivel remains of her body, hanging ravingly from his teeth. It drops just before he reaches into his mouth with terror painted on his fingertips, attempting to the life he unwillingly ingested.

Lily leaves his body and walks along the riverside, collecting the lives of lovers. Just as she was robbed of her first. Those who are undeserving of a fifth, a fifteenth, a twentieth kiss. Once again she finds herself unable to breathe, powerless and captive under the weight of the water—arms floating languidly in front of her, eyelashes decorated with tiny saturated pearls.

———

It's sundown at the riverside. A man with a blanket tucked under his arm walks to the edge of the water.

"Here, Eve! I found a spot!"

Eve walks hurried toward her husband's voice. She stands still and gazes at the water while her husband spreads the blanket on the grass. She shifts the weight of the picnic basket from one arm to the other.

"Oh Frank. The lilies are beautiful."

While Eve empties the contents of the basket, Frank kneels and dips his hand into the water. His fingers graze the white of the flowers. He imagines her face as he strokes the delicate softness of the petals. A grail of remembrance. *Lily.*

Frank stands up and wipes his hand on his trousers. He turns to join Eve on the blanket, and he is nose to nose with her. She smiles wickedly as her mouth opens, spewing polluted water. Muck surfaces from her pores. Her moments are unnatural, as if her joints are locked in place. Her head crooks to the left with a sudden jerk.

The wretched stench of decay is all around him. He stares into her eyes intently, clouded with fear, but well enough to know that the eyes he is gazing into are no longer Eve's.

She puts her hands on either side of his head and draws it close to hers.

He doesn't fight her.

And as if obeying a silent command, an understanding of sorts, he opens his mouth.

Their lips meet and consensually grow wider, as if passing something between them. He feels his insides shrivel and wilt. He finds the strength to push her away, and pounds on his chest, attempting to draw air from the nothingness she's left for him.

Lily steps back and watches him fall to the ground, without a single breath to spare. She steps over him and walks breathlessly toward the riverbank.

MEET THE EDITOR

Steve Capone Jr. (he or they), a Rust Belt native, Autistic creator, and award-winning Utah-based writer, founded Whisper House Press in 2024. This indie horror press released its first horror anthologies, *Costs of Living* and *Dread Mondays*, in the fall of 2025. His latest espionage fiction novel, *Jimmy vs. Communism*, is currently under contract, and is set to build on the success of his 2024 self-published debut, *Max in the Capital of Spies*, which earned him the League of Utah Writers Gold Quill Award for top MA/YA novel.

A versatile author, Steve's work spans genres. He co-edited *Tricks & Treats: A Romance and Horror Microfiction Anthology* (2024), co-edited and helped to guide the Diamond Valley Writers Guild's first anthology *Menagerie: A Compilation of Stories, Poems, and Musings,* and runs WhisperHousePress.com, from which this volume's stories are drawn.

Steve's short fiction can be found in numerous anthologies and literary magazines, including "Driving Angry Opens Doors" (*No Exit*, 2025), "Remission" (*Collective Madness*, 2026), and three pieces in *Darkness 102* (Fall 2025). Other notable short works include "In My Suit" (*Piker Press*, 2025), "Livelihood" (*Ghostlight Magazine*, forthcoming), "Best Friend" (*This Isn't The Place*, 2024), and "Invitation to Eternity" (*Timber Ghost Press*, 2024). He also published his own collection, *That Was Weird: Three Short Stories by Steve Capone Jr* (2024).

Steve is also an accomplished, if early-career, screenwriter. His short screenplay "Cure for Creativity" won Best Short Screenplay at the Bloody Mirror Film Festival in 2024, and was an official selection or finalist at many other festivals, including Oregon Screams and the Chicago Horror Film Festival. His latest, "Submission," is currently making the rounds on the festival circuit. It received selections at multiple festivals and placed as a semi-finalist at HorrorFest International and Vail Screenplay Contest and was a finalist in the Vancouver Horror Show Film Festival.

His nonfiction contributions include essays in the *Salt Lake Tribune* ("Teachers Need Guidance [Re: Book Bans in Utah]," 2024) won the Bronze Quill Award from the League of Utah Writers, and his *Education Week Magazine* article, "Dos and Don'ts of Hybrid Teaching" (2021), along with his numerous educational conference appearances, continue to help teachers across the country to teach more effectively.

Recognized for his contributions to the arts, Steve received the Denis Diderot Grant in support of his July 2025 residency at Chateau d'Orquevaux in rural France. He is deeply committed to fostering literary communities throughout Utah, frequently organizing literature-focused events and serving as a proud member of the Horror Writers Association and League of Utah Writers. He's an executive committee board member with the Southern Utah Book Festival, and he welcomes you to join him in Cedar City in October of 2026 for that event. Steve is also a dedicated pizza advocate and a dog helper with Arctic Rescue.

You can find his incorporeal footprint at https://linktr.ee/steve caponejr.

instagram.com/author_steve_capone_jr
facebook.com/SteveCaponeJr
tiktok.com/@steve_capone_jr_author
youtube.com/@WhisperHousePress
bsky.app/profile/whisperhousepress.bsky.social
amazon.com/author/stevecaponejr
goodreads.com/steve_capone_jr_author

MORE FROM WHISPER HOUSE PRESS

Mission: Whisper House Press publishes and promotes horror capturing life's mundane absurdities. We are committed to empowering and lifting diverse voices, to radical transparency and fairness, and to celebrating human creativity.

Core values: Radical Transparency, Respect and Equity for every human being, and Backing the Upstart.

If you loved this collection, which is a strong representation of our vibe, and if you want *more* mundane horror, please consider picking up *Costs of Living*, *Dread Mondays*, and whatever else we've put out since the publication of this volume, including monthly free-to-read shorts featured on www.whisperhousepress.com.

If you loved this collection, please leave us a review wherever you do that sort of thing. Reviews for independent publishers are a huge deal—it's hard to overstate the help you'd be lending us.

Good luck out there.

If you're struggling today and are contemplating harming yourself, call The Suicide and Crisis Lifeline at 988.

We love you.